The Littlest Pebble

Story & Illustrations by Cliff Graham

ISBN: 978-1-7352676-1-6   Paperback

BISAC Category:
JUV039140 JUVENILE FICTION / Social Themes / Self-Esteem & Self-Reliance
JUV039220 JUVENILE FICTION / Social Themes / Values & Virtues

Printed in the United States

PUREpublishing
P.O. Box 818
Malibu, CA 90265

www.purepublishing.org

This story is not only intended for children but anyone trying to find their place in life.

To Lauren, until we see you again, forever.

Once there was a great, flowing river
Winding its way through the countryside.

In the river were many stones and rocks—

GREAT, LARGE ONES

MEDIUM-SIZED ONES

and, of course,

little ones.

Among those **GREAT**, MEDIUM and little ones was
one itsy-bitsy pebble—the "littlest pebble."

The littlest pebble always dreamed
of being a great stone, solid on the riverbed,
strong enough to split the flowing river.

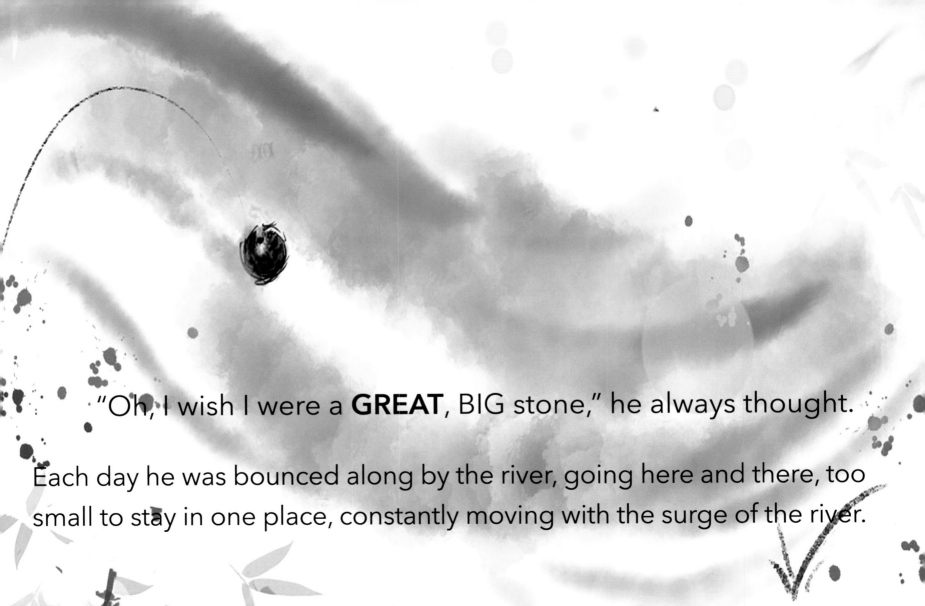

"Oh, I wish I were a **GREAT**, BIG stone," he always thought.

Each day he was bounced along by the river, going here and there, too small to stay in one place, constantly moving with the surge of the river.

"Oh, I wish I were a **GREAT**, BIG stone or even a rock just tumbling a little every time a huge surge of water came. Then, I'd be content," he reasoned.

"Oh, I wish I were a **GREAT**, BIG stone or even a small rock that could lodge between two larger rocks. Then, I wouldn't bounce from bank to bank with no place to stop. I'm really just too small, too little, too much of nothing," he mumbled.

Every day the littlest pebble grumbled on like this.

UNTIL ONE DAY————————WHEN THE RAIN FELL!

This was no ordinary rain. This was a **GREAT, FANTASTIC RAIN**——pouring night and day, on and on.

The river ROSE… AND ROSE… **AND ROSE**.

Soon, it was overflowing its banks, and the littlest pebble was being BoUnCeD and *swirled* and TuMbLeD more than ever.

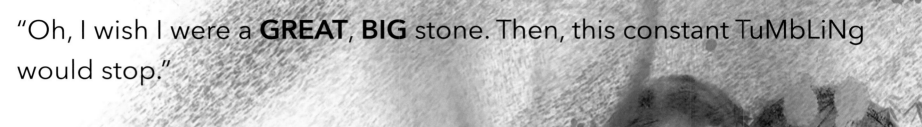

"Oh, I wish I were a **GREAT**, **BIG** stone. Then, this constant TuMbLiNg would stop."

But the GREAT, CONTINUAL RAIN was even pushing around the greatest of rocks. Rocks that had not moved in centuries were being dislodged. They sure didn't bounce around as much as the littlest pebble, but they were moving.

The rocks, stones and pebbles were slowly being pushed downstream. The littlest pebble **BoUnCeD** along quite merrily compared to the others.

Remember... he was used to all this activity.

The river **swelled** beyond recognition.

The littlest pebble didn't know that much further away…at the mouth of the river… there was a town that was in danger. Usually, the river filled a pool where the townspeople got their water. The water was also used to irrigate the land. But now…with the constant rain, the pool had begun to overflow, threatening to flood the town and the entire plain surrounding it.

Only the stones and rocks could help the town now!

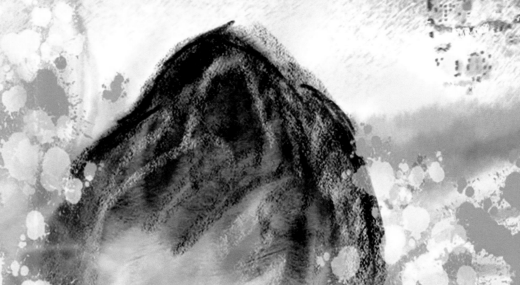

In the meantime... the littlest pebble mused, "Oh, I wish I were a **GREAT** stone then I would be in front, changing the course of the river. Oh, I wish I were a **GREAT**, BIG stone. What good could I do!"

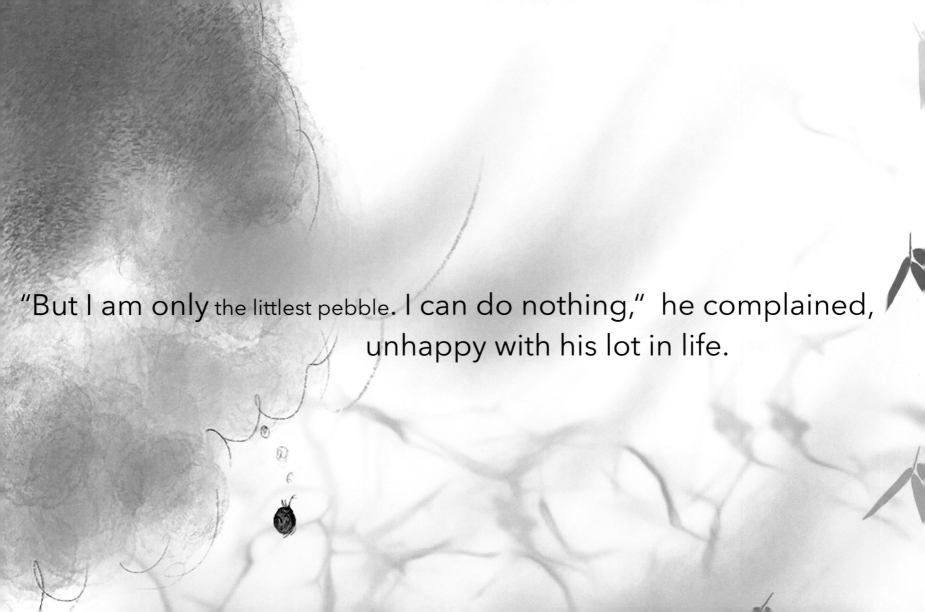

"But I am only the littlest pebble. I can do nothing," he complained, unhappy with his lot in life.

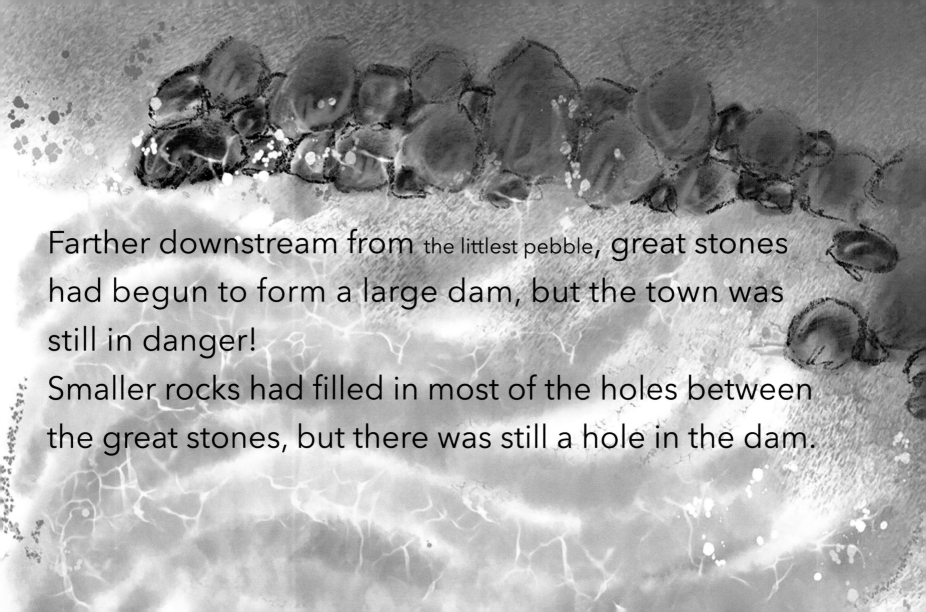

Farther downstream from the littlest pebble, great stones had begun to form a large dam, but the town was still in danger!

Smaller rocks had filled in most of the holes between the great stones, but there was still a hole in the dam.

It was too small of a space for any of the other rocks to fit in. The rocks were beginning to shift —

Oh! What was going to happen to the town and all of its people?

Time and time again, smaller rocks tried to fill the hole, but they were too big.

And then here came the littlest pebble!

"Oh, I wish I were a **GREAT** stone. Then, I would really be something," daydreamed the littlest pebble.

At that moment the littlest pebble did not know that it was hurtling toward its destiny! Hundreds of rocks were attempting to fill the one little space in the dam that would finish the job and save the town.

The littlest pebble TuMbLeD, JuMbLeD ar

"Oh, I wish I were a **GREAT**, LARGE

Suddenly, the commotion ahead caug

Stone after stone,

Rock after rock,

and pebble aft

tried to fill th

OLLED, oblivious to all around it.

one," mused the littlest pebble.

attention as

ebble

y-bitsy spot that had to be filled.

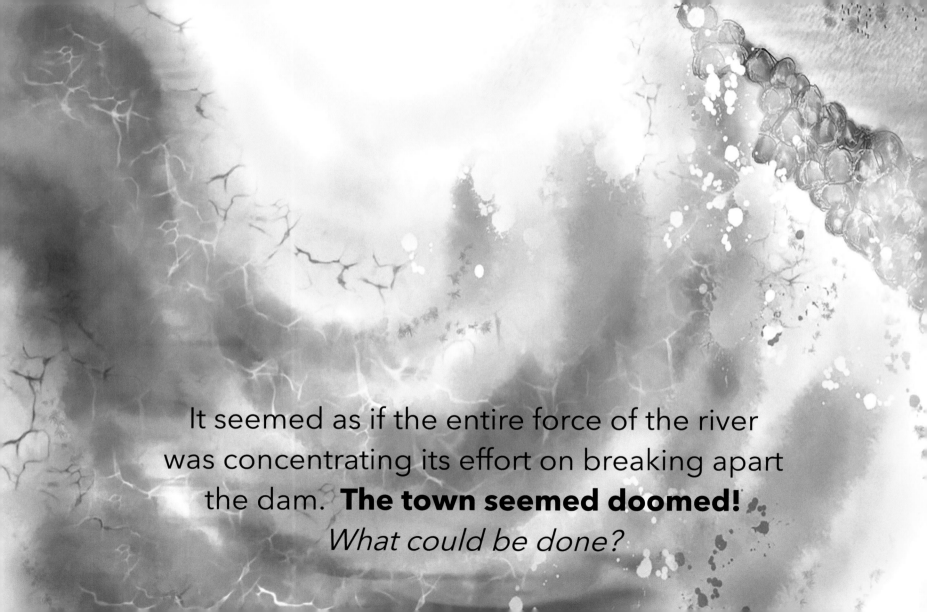

It seemed as if the entire force of the river was concentrating its effort on breaking apart the dam. **The town seemed doomed!** *What could be done?*

"Oh, I wish I were a **GREAT** stone," continued the littlest pebble still caught up in its daydreams.

When suddenly, the littlest pebble saw a hole in the dam—a hole that was directly in front of him, a hole that was too small for the other rocks but a hole that could only be filled by a tiny, little pebble. YES, even perhaps the littlest pebble!

BoUnCiNg toward the hole, the littlest pebble

was **AMAZED**!!

As it **BoUnCeD**, **TuMbLeD** and T𝓌𝒾𝓇𝓁𝑒d toward the hole, the littlest pebble's tune began to change.

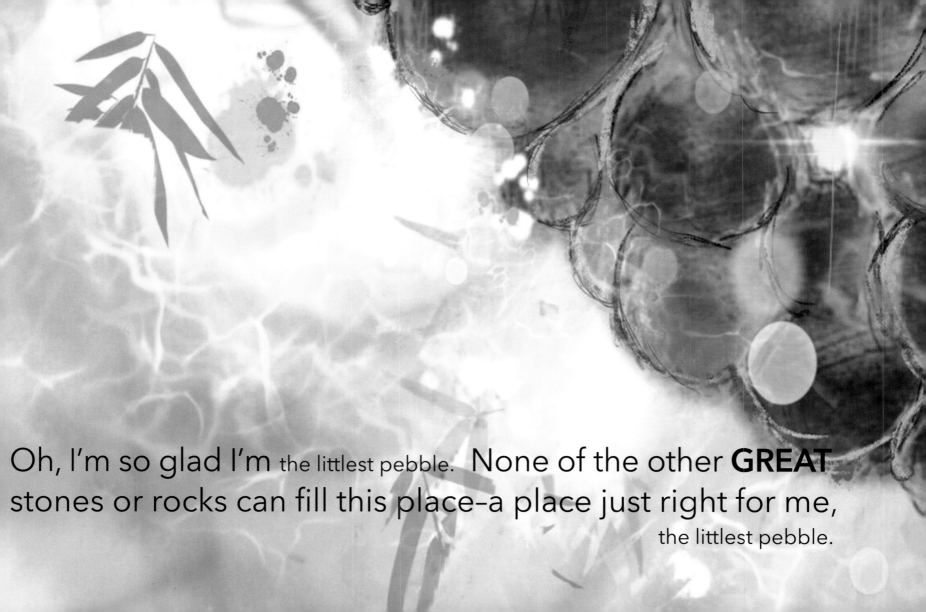

Oh, I'm so glad I'm the littlest pebble. None of the other **GREAT** stones or rocks can fill this place–a place just right for me, the littlest pebble.

The littlest pebble found that it fit just right. The dam wa

ompleted, and the river began to **create a large pool.**

THE TOWN WAS SAVED FROM THE FLOODWATERS ALL BECAUSE OF THE LITTLEST PEBBLE.

The littlest pebble's purpose had indeed been found at the perfect time and in the perfect place—a spot only the littlest pebble could fit.

THE END

Look for other books by the Graham family like *Tori's Terrific Tours*, available at www.lalasgift.org or www.unisonharvest.com.

About the Author and Illustrator

    Cliff Graham has traveled to over 50 nations, being committed to reaching students and their leaders around the world. He loves to see young people fulfill the dreams that God uniquely created them to do. Personable and enthusiastic, Cliff enjoys surfing, skiing, snowboarding, creating art and learning new languages. Above all that, though, Cliff is passionate about having time with his wife Christie and their daughters, Victoria and Alexis.

Cliff_Unisonharvest